Volcanoes and Giant Tarantulas

by Gail Blasser Riley

illustrated by Dominic Bugatto

MODERN CURRICULUM PRESS

Pearson Learning Group

"Mita, it came. We won! We won the contest."

Ernesto dashed out to the garage clutching a letter. Then he watched his collie pounce at the cuffs of his blue jeans.

Ernesto's grandmother jumped up from the motorcycle she was working on. "I told you Salsa was a beautiful dog. I had high expectations, but I didn't think she'd win the '1958 Your Dog Could Be in Movies' contest." Mita pushed her white-streaked black bangs out of her eyes with the back of her hand.

"You know what this means, Mita. We win the trip to Hollywood. And I'll finally get the chance to visit a special-effects studio. Do you think they'll fly us there, Mita? A drive in the car from Texas to California would take forever. It could be scorching. And do you think our old car can make it there?"

3

"Ernesto," said Mita, knitting her brows, "our Rambler rolled off the assembly line only six years ago, in 1952. It's still a very good car."

"I guess so," said Ernesto. "Well, I just hope it doesn't let us down."

"It will be fine, Ernesto," said Mita. "In the meantime, we'd better get busy planning our trip." Mita wiped the oil from her face and hands with a rag.

Ernesto laughed at the oil smudge across her forehead.

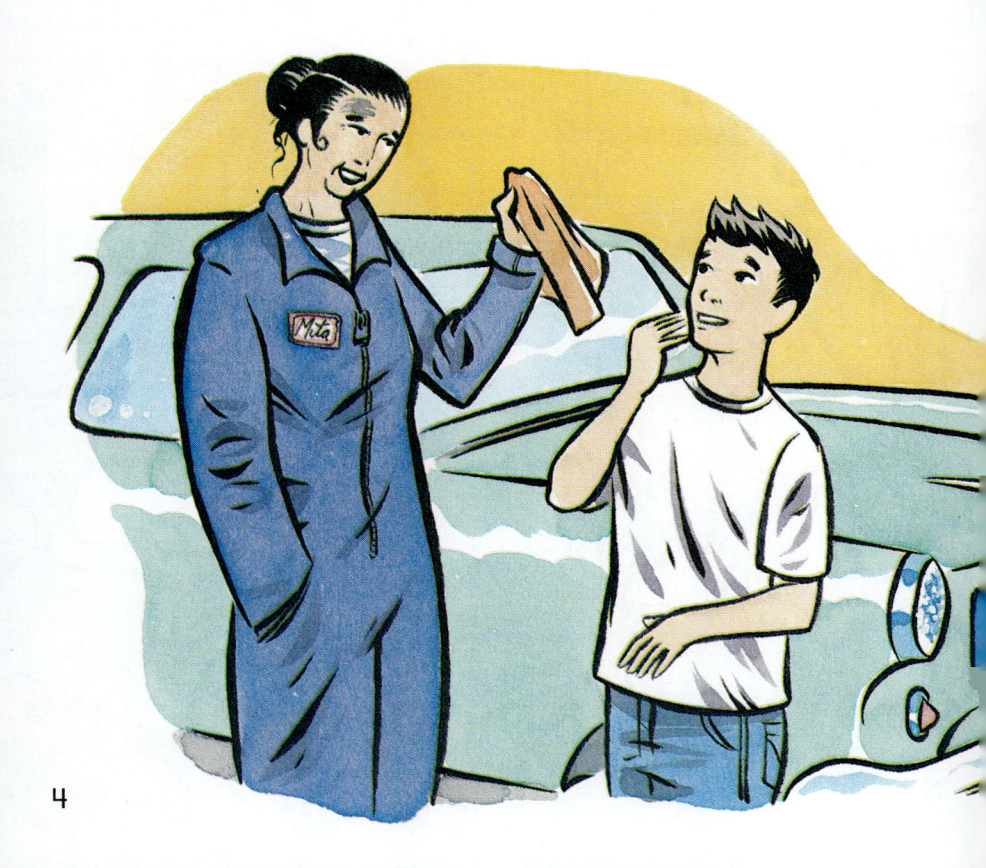

Three weeks flew by. At the airport, Ernesto put Salsa in her carrier. "Mita, she's never been on a plane before. Do you think she'll be okay?" Ernesto asked, wringing his hands.

"You've never been on an airplane before either, and you'll be fine," replied Mita, patting Ernesto on the back.

"But I'm riding in the seats. The regulations say that Salsa has to ride in a compartment below us." Ernesto gritted his teeth.

"You'll see," said Mita. "She will be just fine. She may even make friends with other pets in their cages in that compartment. When we get to California, Salsa will race out of the carrier and pounce on you, just as she always does."

As the plane took off, Mita asked Ernesto, "Are you nervous about this trip? It would only be natural."

"Are you kidding?" Ernesto shot back. "This is about the greatest thing I've ever done." Ernesto leaned back and cupped his hands behind his head as he let out a huge sigh and settled back into his seat. He watched the billowy clouds outside the window as they seemed to swallow the plane.

"This is only the first step, Mita," he said. "One day, I'll work in Hollywood. I'll work on TV shows and movies with special effects. I'll create the animation in movies. And I'll come up with new concepts to make film monsters. The special-effects studio—that's the part of this trip I'm looking forward to the most. It will be nice to take Salsa to the movie set, but more than anything, I want to go see the special effects. Do you have the schedule, Mita? Which day do we spend at the special-effects studio?"

Ernesto smiled boldly at Mita, but as she answered, he didn't even hear her words. Instead, his own words echoed in his ears: "I'll work on TV shows and movies with special effects." Ernesto's insides quivered like a bowl of jelly. Beads of perspiration welled up on his forehead. He knew he talked a good game, but he also knew that every time he came close to catching a dream, he fell apart. He always felt he was about to knock something over or break something or ask all the wrong questions. And if he had a chance to make something of his own, he was afraid he'd destroy that chance too.

"Ernesto!" Mita shook Ernesto's shoulders. "We're here. The plane's landing."

"Sorry, Mita," Ernesto said. "I must have dozed off."

8

Ernesto thought it would take forever for everyone to get off of the plane, but soon he and Mita stepped into the airport.

"First stop, our contest winner!" said Ernesto.

He and Mita headed to claim Salsa. Salsa bounded out of the carrier and jumped almost as high as Ernesto's shoulder. Mita clasped a leash onto Salsa's collar.

The first couple of days of the trip were great. Ernesto enjoyed the visit to the set of a TV show, but he knew he was really just marking time until he could go to the special-effects studio.

"Tomorrow," he said aloud, as he drifted off to sleep the night before the scheduled visit.

The next morning, Ernesto awoke to the mellow aroma of Mita's coffee. He rubbed his eyes as he sat up and looked around the hotel room. Salsa hopped up on the bed and licked his face.

"Morning, girl," he said, as he stroked her long coat and scratched her belly.

"I thought you'd be up and raring to go by now," said Mita, handing him a glass of orange juice.

"How much time do we have?" asked Ernesto.

"About an hour—and it's only ten minutes away," answered Mita.

Ernesto chewed his lip. He'd been waiting for a day like this for about as long as he could remember. Part of him wanted to jump out of bed and race out of the room to head for the special-effects studio, but another part of him wanted to crawl back under the covers and hide. Neither part had the courage to tell Mita he was nervous about going. So he slid out of bed, got ready, and ambled outside to wait for the taxicab with Mita and Salsa.

"That's quite a dog you have there," said the cab driver as Salsa jumped in the back seat with Ernesto and Mita.

Ernesto slid into the cab, glad to be out of the scorching California sun.

"Thanks," said Ernesto. "I guess you could almost say this is more her trip than ours."

"Why do you say that?" asked the driver.

"She won a contest," said Ernesto, "a 'Your Dog Could Be in Movies' contest."

"You're the boy I read about in the paper the other morning," said the cab driver. "They flew you all the way out here from Houston. To the town where people make dreams happen, the article said. Didn't you win a visit to Chang's special-effects studio as part of the prize?"

"We did," said Ernesto. "That's where we're headed now."

"You're in for quite a treat," the driver replied. "Have you ever seen pictures of Chang's studio or read any of the articles about him?"

"I've seen a few pictures," said Ernesto. "But what's the studio like? And what's Mr. Chang like?"

"Chang's probably one of the most amazing fellows you'll ever meet. He started showing his own work in art shows when he was younger than you are. He went to work for a major studio when he was only twenty-one. He was the youngest person who'd ever worked in the Special Effects and Models Department."

"What did he work on there?" asked Ernesto.

"He made wooden models to show animators how different figures moved."

"What else did he do?" asked Ernesto.

"Here he is. You can ask him yourself," said the driver as the cab pulled into a long driveway.

Mita stepped out of the cab. Salsa followed. Ernesto's heart pounded. He shrank down into the seat. *I'm so nervous about meeting someone this famous,* he thought. *I hope I don't do something wrong. I feel like hiding.* But there was nowhere to hide. Salsa tugged gently at Ernesto's hand.

Then a thin man with a broad smile peeked inside the cab.

"Ernesto," he said, "It's a pleasure to meet you. I'm Wah Chang."

Ernesto opened his mouth, but no words came out. Chang extended his hand. Ernesto shook it and slowly eased his way out of the cab. Then Ernesto noticed that Mr. Chang limped when he walked. He figured Mr. Chang could hear his thoughts, because Chang said, "I had polio, when I was younger. But I get around just fine now."

"Pleased to meet you, sir," Ernesto finally managed.

Inside the studio, Ernesto marveled at all the people and activity. He jumped back and gasped when a giant hairy spider leg brushed the top of his head.

"Where did that come from?" he asked, as he gazed up at the most realistic-looking tarantula he'd ever seen—realistic, that is, except for its size. Its furry four-foot-long body, complete with beady eyes, hung from the ceiling. Its dangling legs must have been at least five feet long.

"We worked on a film a while back about giant tarantulas," said Chang. "We used tarantulas this size for some of the scenes. For other scenes, we built a tiny town and used live tarantulas, about fifty of them. The strange thing was, when we finished filming, we could never account for two real ones. Actually, we shot the scenes in that studio." Chang pointed to a nearby door.

Ernesto's eyes grew wide. He scanned the huge room from side to side, but saw nothing furry scurrying along the floor—except Salsa—and that was just fine.

"Mr. Chang," he asked, as he noticed pictures of elaborate masks on the wall. "I think I've seen those before, but I can't remember where. Did you make those for a movie?"

"Yes, and they looked great," said Chang, smiling.

This time, even Mita's eyes grew wide. "They're beautiful, Mr. Chang," she said.

"I'm filming a scene for a new movie about time travel today," said Chang. "Would you like to be my guest for the filming?"

Ernesto's heart pounded. His dream was just around the corner, much closer than he'd imagined. His teeth chattered with anxiety. "Would it be all right, Mita?" asked Ernesto, excited and terrified at the same time.

"It's fine," said Mita.

"Let me give you some background," said Chang. "In this scene, the star of the film has traveled through time and finds himself at the site of a volcanic eruption."

"Does the volcano actually erupt in the scene?" asked Ernesto.

"Absolutely!" said Chang.

"How do you make it look real?" This was a question Ernesto had considered many times as he'd dreamed up special effects himself.

"We considered many different ways to make it look real. But we finally settled on using oatmeal."

"Oatmeal?" asked Ernesto. "Why oatmeal?"

"It has about the same consistency as lava, and if you add red dye—and film it under red lights—it looks like the real thing. We built ramps into the set, so that the 'lava' will flow naturally."

As they entered a small studio, Chang turned to Mita. "No space for dogs. Do you mind waiting out here?"

"Not at all," answered Mita.

As Ernesto stepped inside, he was shocked to find the room was only about half the size of his classrooms at school. Scorching hot lights blazed above a miniature town, and technical crew members worked behind it. Two cameras were set up in front of the miniature town.

"The oatmeal is up there, above the set in containers. We cooked up about 250 gallons of it last Friday. Just to be on the safe side, we covered the set in heavy plastic that doesn't show on film. That way, if there's a problem, we'll be able to pull up the plastic, set the shot, and film again—without building an entirely new set." Chang smiled.

Ernesto took a close look at the cameras. *Hope I don't knock one over*, he thought, as he took a step back and winced. *I'd better be careful. I could completely destroy this shot. Then I'd probably be banned from Hollywood forever.* Ernesto's pulse quickened.

Maybe Chang sensed his anxiety. "You know, I was just a little bit younger than you are when I started showing my art. At first, people didn't take me seriously. But I knew what I wanted to do. I had a dream to create, and nothing could make me give up my dream."

Ernesto thought he caught a twinkle in Chang's eye. He knew that Mr. Chang meant well, but now Ernesto was more nervous than ever.

"Quiet on the set," someone yelled. "Take one!"

Ernesto's jaw dropped. He froze in his spot. He dared not move a muscle. *It wouldn't matter if this were a real volcano erupting real lava,* he thought, *because I couldn't move. I'd just have to stand here and be swallowed up.*

"Oh, no," cried Chang.

Ernesto, still glued to his spot, smelled the odor of a million rotten eggs. He gasped as thick, bumpy, red, rotten oatmeal flowed down the ramps—straight for the cameras! What had Chang said about the oatmeal? They'd cooked it up on Friday—three days before! The oatmeal was rotten.

"The plastic!" cried Chang. "It's rolled up off the corners of the set. It'll ruin everything! We won't be able to build another set in time." The crew members stood helpless behind the set. They couldn't get to the plastic covering. Chang and the other special effects man raced to the edge and middle of the set and tugged the plastic, but it was caught under a miniature car near Ernesto.

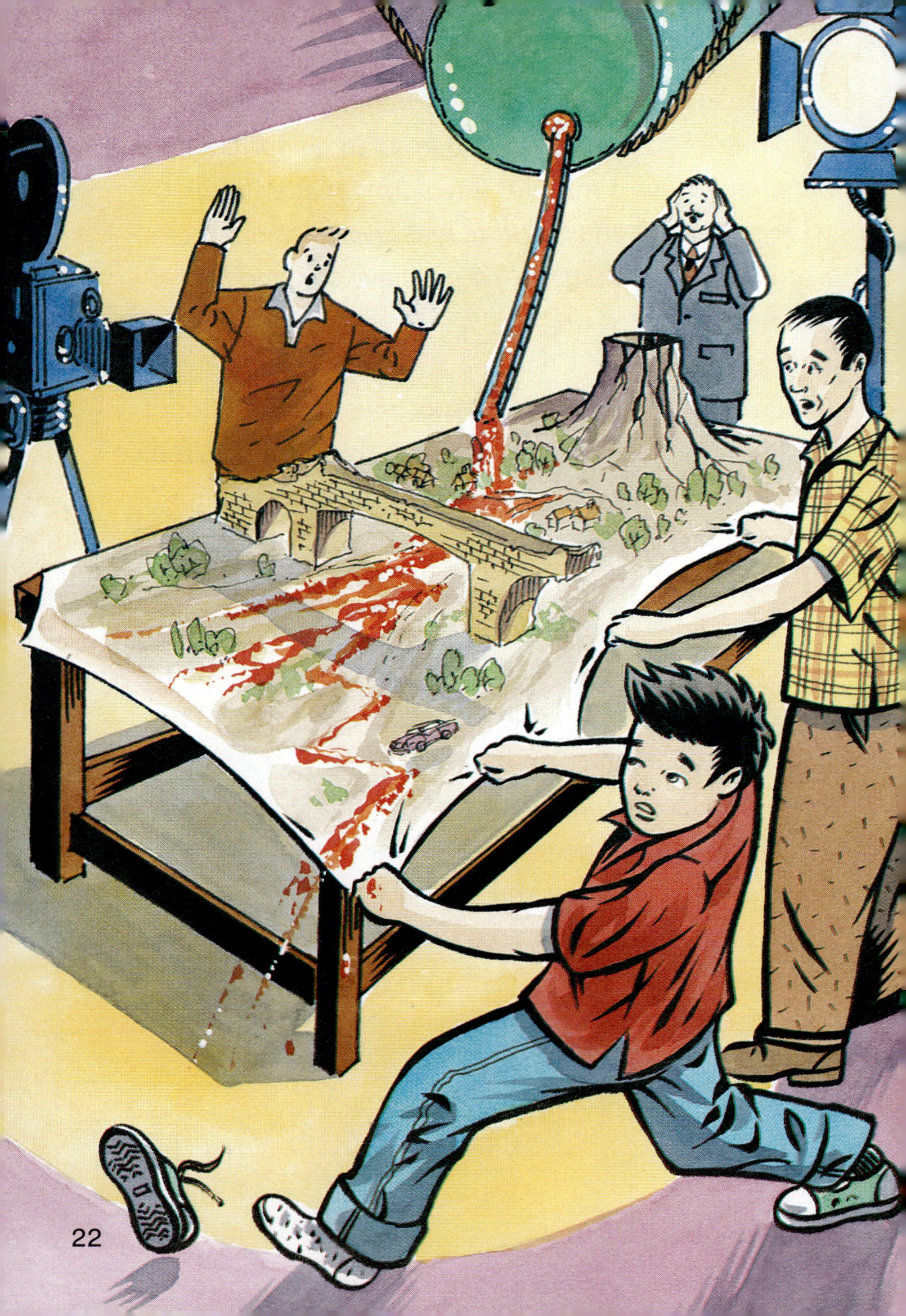

"Ernesto, help! Hurry! Grab the plastic. Pull it back. If I let go here, it'll roll all the way back, and we'll lose the set for sure."

Ernesto's temples pounded. Sweat dripped from his palms. He thought his heart would burst from his chest. He knew it. He'd known all along he'd destroy his dream—and now he was about to be responsible for destroying something else along with it.

"We can't do this without you, Ernesto. We really need you."

I have to do this, thought Ernesto. *I have to pull it together!* He moved one foot. *I feel as if I'm moving in slow motion,* he thought, *but at least I'm moving.* He spun around to grab the plastic and slipped on a film canister. The red globs flowed closer. He heard shouts from all over the room. As he stood up, he tripped over his shoelace, and his sneaker flew off his foot. The red oatmeal lava mess heaved forward, only inches away. Ernesto stretched his body and pulled the plastic forward as the lumpy red oatmeal flowed over his hand.

Cheers arose from the room.

"You've got a job in my studio any time," said Chang as they left the room.

Out in the hall, Salsa jumped into Ernesto's arms.

"I'm glad you're happy," Ernesto said to Salsa. "This whole great experience started with you!"

Salsa barked and everyone laughed.

"What happened in there?" Mita asked.

"Well, Mita, we make dreams happen," said Ernesto, feeling prouder than he had ever felt before.